THE THREE LITTLE JAVELINAS

by Susan Lowell
Illustrated by Jim Harris

SCHOLASTIC INC.
New York Toronto London Auckland Sydney

For Anna, all by herself

ISBN 0-590-48170-3

Copyright © 1992 by Susan Lowell.
Illustrations copyright © 1992 by Jim Harris.
All rights reserved. Published by Scholastic Inc.,
730 Broadway, New York, NY 10003,
by arrangement with Northland Publishing Co.

12 11 10 9 8 7   5 6 7 8 9/9

Printed in the U.S.A.   08

First Scholastic printing, January 1994

This is a southwestern adaptation of a familiar folktale: a chile-flavored "The Three Little Pigs." The story takes place in the Sonoran Desert, where Native American, Mexican, and Anglo cultures blend together.

Javelina (pronounced ha-ve-LEE-na) comes from a Spanish name for the collared peccary, a New World relative of swine (but not a true pig) that ranges from the southwestern United States down to the tip of South America. Javelinas are extremely bristly—very hairy on the chinny-chin-chin. Oddly enough, they are also related to the hippopotamus. In the American Southwest, another common local name for peccaries, besides javelinas, is "wild pigs."

ONCE UPON A TIME,

way out in the desert, there were three little javelinas. Javelinas (ha-ve-LEE-nas) are wild, hairy, southwestern cousins of pigs.

Their heads were hairy, their backs were hairy, and their bony legs—all the way down to their hard little hooves—were very hairy. But their snouts were soft and pink.

One day, the three little javelinas trotted away to seek their fortunes. In this hot, dry land, the sky was almost always blue. Steep purple mountains looked down on the desert, where the cactus forests grew.

Soon the little javelinas came to a spot where the path divided, and each one went a different way.

The first little javelina wandered lazily
along. He didn't see a dust storm
whirling across the desert—until it
caught him.

The whirlwind blew away and left the
first little javelina sitting in a heap of
tumbleweeds. Brushing himself off, he
said, "I'll build a house with them!" And
in no time at all, he did.

Then along came a coyote. He ran through the desert so quickly and so quietly that he was almost invisible. In fact, this was
only one of Coyote's many magical tricks. He laughed when he
saw the tumbleweed house and smelled the javelina inside.

"Mmm! A tender juicy piggy!" he thought. Coyote was tired of
eating mice and rabbits.

He called out sweetly, "Little pig, little pig, let me come in."

"Not by the hair of my chinny-chin-chin!" shouted the first javelina (who had a lot of hair on his chinny-chin-chin!)

"Then I'll huff, and I'll puff, and I'll blow your house in!" said Coyote.

And he huffed, and he puffed, and he blew the little
tumbleweed house away.

But in all the hullabaloo, the first little javelina escaped—
and went looking for his brother and sister.

Coyote, who was very sneaky, tiptoed along behind.

The second little javelina walked for miles among giant cactus plants called saguaros (sa-WA-ros). They held their ripe red fruit high in the sky. But they made almost no shade, and the little javelina grew hot.

Then he came upon a Native American woman who was gathering sticks from inside a dried-up cactus. She planned to use these long sticks, called saguaro ribs, to knock down the sweet cactus fruit.

The second little javelina said, "Please, may I have some sticks to build a house?"

"*Ha'u,*" (Ha-ou) she said, which means "yes" in the language of the Desert People.

When he was finished building his house, he lay down in the shade. Then his brother arrived, panting from the heat, and the second little javelina moved over and made a place for him.

Pretty soon, Coyote found the saguaro rib house. He used his magic to make his voice sound just like another javelina's.

"Little pig, little pig, let me come in!" he called.

But the little javelinas were suspicious. The second one cried, "No! Not by the hair of my chinny-chin-chin!"

"Bah!" thought Coyote. "I am not going to eat your *hair.*"

Then Coyote smiled, showing all his sharp teeth: "I'll huff, and I'll puff, and I'll blow your house in!"

So he huffed, and he puffed, and all the saguaro ribs came tumbling down.

But the two little javelinas escaped into the desert.
Still not discouraged, Coyote followed. Sometimes
his magic did fail, but then he usually came up with
another trick.

The third little javelina trotted through beautiful palo verde trees, with green trunks and yellow flowers. She saw a snake sliding by, smooth as oil. A hawk floated round and round above her. Then she came to a place where a man was making adobe (a-DOE-be) bricks from mud and straw. The bricks lay on the ground, baking in the hot sun.

The third little javelina thought for a moment, and said, "May I please have a few adobes to build a house?"

"*Sí,*" answered the man, which means "yes" in Spanish, the brick-maker's language.

So the third javelina built herself a solid little adobe house, cool in summer and warm in winter. When her brothers found her, she welcomed them in and locked the door behind them.

Coyote followed their trail.

"Little pig, little pig, let me come in!" he called.

The three little javelinas looked out the window. This time Coyote pretended to be very old and weak, with no teeth and a sore paw. But they were not fooled.

"No! Not by the hair of my chinny-chin-chin," called back the third little javelina.

"Then I'll huff, and I'll puff, and I'll blow your house in!" said Coyote. He grinned, thinking of the wild pig dinner to come.

"Just try it!" shouted the third little javelina. So Coyote huffed and puffed, but the adobe bricks did not budge.

Again, Coyote tried. "I'LL HUFF . . . AND I'LL PUFF . . . AND I'LL BLOW YOUR HOUSE IN!"

The three little javelinas covered their hairy ears. But nothing happened. The javelinas peeked out the window.

The tip of Coyote's raggedy tail whisked right past their noses. He was climbing upon the tin roof. Next, Coyote used his magic to make himself very skinny.

"The stove pipe!" gasped the third little javelina. Quickly she lighted a fire inside her wood stove.

"What a feast it will be!" Coyote said to himself. He squeezed into the stove pipe. "I think I'll eat them with red hot chile sauce!"

Whoosh. S-s-sizzle!

Then the three little javelinas heard an amazing noise.
It was not a bark. It was not a cackle. It was not a howl.
It was not a scream. It was all of those sounds together.
"Yip
    yap
     yeep
         YEE-OWW-OOOOOOOOOOOOO!"
Away ran a puff of smoke shaped like a coyote.

The three little javelinas lived happily ever after in the adobe house.

And if you ever hear Coyote's voice, way out in the desert at night . . . well, you know what he's remembering!

A NOTE ON THE STORY

In addition to the classic European-American tale, my sources include the many Coyote fables told by southwestern Indians, particularly those of the Tohono O'Odham, (toe-HO-no O-OH-tam) or Desert People, formerly known as the Papago tribe, of southern Arizona and northern Mexico. In these stories, Coyote is always a laugher and a trickster who is frequently outsmarted by the other animals.

The setting for this story is the vicinity of the Tohono O'Odham Reservation, near Tucson, Arizona, in early summer. At this time of year, the saguaro cactus flowers start to bear fruit, which the Tohono O'Odham harvest by knocking them down with long sticks, called saguaro ribs, the "skeletons" of the fallen giant cacti. (The fruit is still used to brew a sacred wine for the annual rain-making ceremony.) It's also a good season to see dust storms, thunderheads, and baby javelinas looking like homely, hairy loaves of bread on hooves.

The pigs' houses in this story fit the southwestern theme as well: the Tohono O'Odham traditionally built temporary brush shelters, as well as more permanent homes of sticks and mud, and ramadas (roofs without walls) just for shade. Mud adobe houses, built with local adobes and topped with tin roofs, are still in use across the Southwest.

In this story, I have tried to handle all this geographical and cultural material with a light touch. The setting could really be almost any dry southwestern area where javelinas, coyotes, tumbleweeds, cacti, and adobe houses are found—which includes parts of Texas, New Mexico, Arizona, and California, as well as northern Mexico.

ABOUT THE AUTHOR

SUSAN LOWELL spends part of her time in Tucson, Arizona, and part of it on a small ranch in the desert, where she sees javelinas and coyotes from her windows. (The ranch house is made of stone—with a tin roof.) She has written a book for adults, *Ganado Red: A Novella and Stories*, but this is her first children's book. She and her husband have two young daughters.

ABOUT THE ILLUSTRATOR

JIM HARRIS lives with his wife and two children near Mesa, Colorado, on the north face of the largest flat-topped mountain in the world. His house is at the end of a dirt road, where the coyotes howl every night and elk sometimes walk on the deck of his studio. He has been an artist since the age of four, but has been paid for his work since 1981.